This book is given to:

_____

from:

_____

Dedication

In memory of Karen Farley,
who taught me how to type and—
through her life and love—taught me
how to be more ThoughtFull.

Published by B&H Publishing Group,
Nashville, Tennessee

All Scripture quotations are taken from the Christian
Standard Bible®, Copyright © 2017 by Holman Bible Publishers.
Used by permission. Christian Standard Bible® and CSB® are
federally registered trademarks of Holman Bible Publishers.

DEWEY: C177   SBHD: THOUGHTFULNESS \ FRIENDSHIP \ HANDICAPPED CHILDREN

Printed in April 2018 in Shenzhen, Guangdong, China

1 2 3 4 5 6 · 22 21 20 19 18

ThoughtFull

Discovering the Unique Gifts in Each of Us

Dorena Williamson

Illustrated by Robert Dunn

B&H
PUBLISHING GROUP
Nashville, Tennessee

"Good morning, everyone! It's that time again," started Dr. Campo. "Time for . . . "

"HEART awards!" shouted the students.

Everyone began to chant together.

"H is for Hardworking. That means never quit.

E is for Excellence. That means do your best.

A is for Adventurous. That means try new things.

R is for Respect. That means listen up.

T is for Thoughtful. That means others first!"

"Great job!" said Dr. Campo. "I'm very proud of the young man who gets the Heart award today. Among his unique gifts, he always looks out for his friends and helps anyone he can. He is an example we can all look up to.

"I am pleased to present the Thoughtful award to . . . Ahanu Robinson!"

The second-grade class cheered with excitement. Ahanu was such a good friend to them all.

At the end of the day, it was time to board the buses.
Ahanu was still excited about his award, and Joshua
was sure to congratulate him.

But on the bus, Joshua heard some boys talking behind him.

"His name is weird—'Ahanu'?"

"Yeah, he acts different too. Why did he get a stupid award anyway?"

Joshua's heart sank. He didn't like hearing what the boys said about his friend.

Ahanu soon jumped off the bus at his house. "Look, look, Mama Siouxsan!" He pressed his Heart award into his grandma's hands.

"Well, what is this, Ahanu?" she asked.

"I got an award today. And they all clapped for me!"

"Well, this is just wonderful," said Mama Siouxsan with a smile. "I've got a snack ready. You can tell me all about it."

Joshua was quiet as he walked toward his front door. "How was your day, son? Ready to shoot some hoops?" asked his dad.

"We had the Heart awards today. Ahanu got the award for being thoughtful," replied Joshua.

"That's exciting!" said Dad. "But you don't look very happy about it. What's wrong?"

"I'm happy for Ahanu," said Joshua. "It's just, well, on the bus, some boys said some mean things about him."

"I'm sorry, son. That was wrong. How did it make you feel?" asked Dad.

"It made me really sad," said Joshua. "Ahanu is nice to everyone. Our whole class was really happy for him. Except those bullies."

"I'm glad you were one of the ones cheering for Ahanu," Dad said. "Billions of people live in the world, and each one of us has value. If we only spend time around people who are like us, we miss out on discovering the unique things about people who are different from us. The truth is, we're all gifted by God's design.

"Tell me, what unique gifts does Ahanu have?"

Joshua thought for a moment. "In art class, Ahanu works really hard at painting, and you can tell 'cause he's really good. And on the playground, when you give him the football, he loves to run down the field."

"And you know what? Ahanu pats people on the back all the time and encourages them. Sometimes I'm full of worries or selfish thoughts. But Ahanu is always full of good thoughts—about everybody! No wonder he's known for being thoughtFULL."

Joshua's dad smiled. "I'm proud of you, Joshua," he said.

"You know all this about Ahanu because you are thoughtful too.
Those boys on the bus only see him as a boy with Down syndrome.
But you see a kind friend who tries really hard at everything he does."

"Imagine if we all did that," Dad continued. "If kids and adults worked at discovering the unique gifts in other people, we could all be thoughtFULL, just like Ahanu!"

"Yeah! Dr. Campo told us we should
look up to Ahanu," said Joshua.
"I think you already do," said Dad.

The next day at school, Joshua spoke to the boys he had heard on the bus. "Hey, guys, have you ever seen Ahanu run the football or paint in art class?"

"Not really," they replied.

"Well, he's my friend, and he's really good at both those things! Plus, he's always being kind and thinking about ways to help people. That's why he won the Thoughtful award. We could all learn a lot from him."

At recess, Joshua looked for Ahanu. "Hey," Joshua began,
"want me to push you on the swing?"

"Yep, let's go!" answered Ahanu. He ran to his favorite
tire swing.

"I gotta sit criss-cross-applesauce!" he said. He looked at Joshua. "Thank you," he said with a smile.

"Any time," said Joshua. "I may not be as good with a paintbrush, Ahanu, but when it comes to being thoughtFULL, I'm going to try to be just like you!"

Remember:

Now there are different gifts, but the same Spirit.—1 Corinthians 12:4

Read:

Read 1 Corinthians 12:12–31. God made the human body with many unique parts, and each one has a special job. Some of those parts are small and loud (like the mouth), some are big and strong (like the legs), and other important parts are quiet and hidden (like the heart and lungs). But all the parts work together to keep the body healthy.

Similarly, God calls His people the "body of Christ." That means we are connected, and each of us has a special gift, a job to do to keep the body of Christ strong. Those gifts are different yet valuable. God has given each of us unique talents, and we should work to discover and celebrate both the visible and hidden gifts in each of us!

Think:

1. Think about your body. How does it all work together? Which parts are hidden but important?

2. Ahanu is excited to receive the Heart award. How would you feel if you were given a special award?

3. The bullies said mean words about Ahanu, and that made Joshua sad. Have you seen someone be bullied? How did you feel?

4. In the story, God gave Ahanu the gift of being *full* of good thoughts about others. How does Ahanu inspire you to be more thought*full*?

5. Ahanu has Down syndrome. Joshua's dad reminds us to see the value God placed in *every* person, including friends like Ahanu who are differently abled in how their bodies work. Why is it important to remember we are all valuable?